WITHDRAWN

Wilmington Public Library District
201 S. Kankakee St.
Wilmington, IL 60481
(815) 476-2834

My Whiskers Are Long and White

by Jessica Rudolph

**Consultant:
Christopher Kuhar, PhD
Executive Director
Cleveland Metroparks Zoo
Cleveland, Ohio**

New York, New York

Credits
Cover, © mary416/Shutterstock; 4–5, © asavliuk/iStock; 6–7, © Tereshchenko Dmitry/Shutterstock; 8–9, © Juhku/Dreamstime; 10–11, © Abeselom Zerit/Shutterstock; 12–13, © cddonaldson/Shutterstock; 14–15, © TOMO/Shutterstock; 16–17, © tristan tan/Shutterstock; 18–19, © WILDLIFE GmbH/Alamy Stock Photo; 20–21, © WILDLIFE GmbH/Alamy Stock Photo; 22, © esdeem/Shutterstock; 23, © Eric Isselee/Shutterstock; 24, © Eric Isselee/Shutterstock.

Publisher: Kenn Goin
Editor: J. Clark
Creative Director: Spencer Brinker
Design: Debrah Kaiser

Library of Congress Cataloging-in-Publication Data in process at time of publication (2017)
Library of Congress Control Number: 2016007669
ISBN-13: 978-1-944102-61-6

Copyright © 2017 Bearport Publishing Company, Inc. All rights reserved. No part of this publication may be reproduced in whole or in part, stored in any retrieval system, or transmitted in any form or by any means, electronic, mechanical, photocopying, recording, or otherwise, without written permission from the publisher.

For more information, write to Bearport Publishing Company, Inc., 45 West 21st Street, Suite 3B, New York, New York 10010. Printed in the United States of America.

10 9 8 7 6 5 4 3 2 1

Contents

What Am I? 4
Animal Facts 22
Where Do I Live? 23
Index 24
Read More 24
Learn More Online 24
About the Author 24

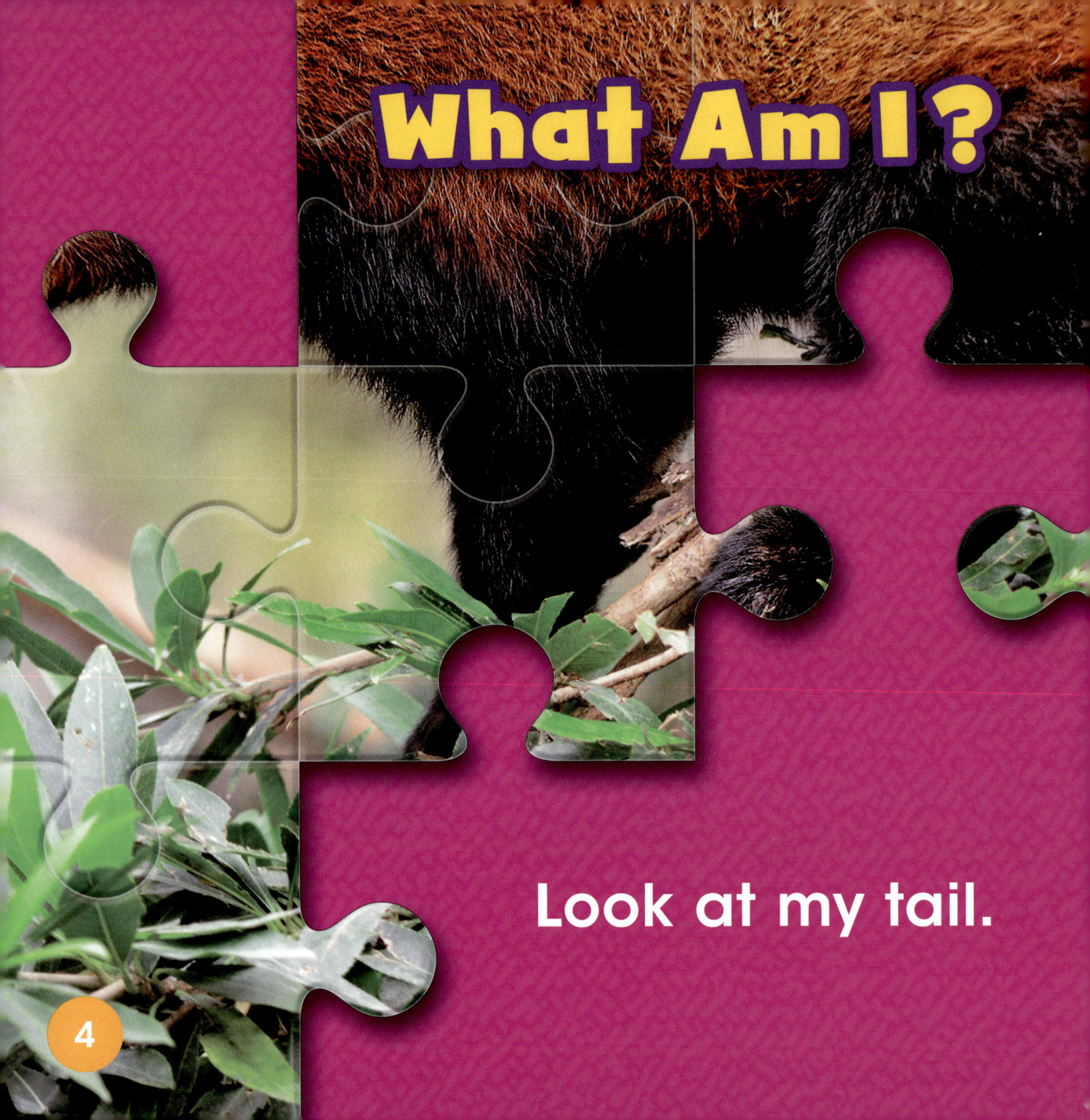

What Am I?

Look at my tail.

It is long and striped.

The fur on my body is red.

It is very soft.

I have four legs.

They are short and black.

My whiskers are long and white.

My ears are shaped like triangles.

They are fuzzy, too.

I have sharp claws.

14

My tongue is pink.

It feels rough.

What am I?

Let's find out!

I am a red panda!

Animal Facts

Red pandas are more closely related to raccoons and skunks than they are to giant pandas. Like almost all mammals, red pandas give birth to live young that drink milk.

More Red Panda Facts

Food:	Mostly bamboo but also fruit, acorns, and bird eggs
Size:	Up to 46 inches (1.2 m) long, including the tail
Weight:	Up to 16 pounds (7.3 kg)
Life Span:	About 10 years in the wild
Cool Fact:	Because of its red fur, the Chinese name for the red panda is *hun-ho*, which means "fire fox."

Adult Red Panda Size

Where Do I Live?

Red pandas live in the mountains of Asia. They spend most of their time in trees.

Index

claws 14–15
ears 12–13
fur 6–7, 13, 22
legs 8–9
tail 4–5, 22
tongue 16–17
whiskers 10–11

Read More

Miller, Sara Swan. *Red Pandas (Paws and Claws).* New York: PowerKids Press (2008).

Roumanis, Alexis. *I Am a Red Panda.* New York: Weigl (2015).

Learn More Online

To learn more about red pandas, visit
www.bearportpublishing.com/ZooClues

About the Author

Jessica Rudolph lives in Connecticut. She has edited and written many books about history, science, and nature for children.